TOUCHED
BY AN
ANGEL

A Delicate Balance

P9-DGS-864

"Rebecca, you landed perfectly," said Monica. "The only thing missing was a smile."

TOUCHED
BY AN
ANGEL

A Delicate Balance

Written by Monica Hall
Based on a teleplay by
Debbie Smith and Danna Doyle
from a story by Jennifer Wharton

Martha Williamson
Executive Producer

Based on the television
series created by
John Masius

Thomas Nelson, Inc.
Nashville

A Delicate Balance
Book One in the *Touched By An Angel* fiction series.

A Delicate Balance by Monica Hall is based on a teleplay by Debbie Smith and Danna Doyle from a story by Jennifer Wharton.

Published in Nashville, Tennessee, by Tommy Nelson™, a division of Thomas Nelson, Inc. Executive Editor: Laura Minchew; Managing Editor: Beverly Phillips.

Library of Congress Cataloging-in-Publication Data

Hall, Monica.
    A delicate balance / written by Monica Hall : based on a teleplay
  by Debbie Smith and Danna Doyle : from a story by Jennifer Wharton.
      p. cm.—(Touched by an angel)
    Summary: As Rebecca prepares for a big gymnastics competition, she, her brother, and their mother all need the help of three angels in coping with stress and the recent death of their father.
    ISBN 0-8499-5802-4
    [1. Gymnastics—Fiction. 2. Guardian angels—Fiction. 3. Angels—Fiction. 4. Brothers and sisters—Fiction. 5. Death—Fiction.]
    I. Smith, Debbie. II. Doyle, Danna. III. Wharton, Jennifer.
    IV. Touched by an angel (Television program) V. Title. VI. Series.
PZ7.H14725Dg 1998
[Fic]—dc21

                                 98-11483
                                 CIP
                                 AC

Printed in the United States of America
98 99 00 01 DHC 9 8 7 6 5 4 3 2 1

Contents

Contents

The Characters

Rebecca Browner, a talented fourteen-year-old gymnast, who has a lot to learn about what makes a true champion.

Peter Browner, Rebecca and T. J.'s father, who died of cancer.

Sandra Browner, Rebecca's mother, who tries so hard to keep a dream alive that she forgets what keeps a family together.

T. J. Browner, Rebecca's daredevil twelve-year-old brother, who is still very hurt and angry about his father's death.

Nadia Comaneci, a Romanian gymnast who received an unprecedented perfect score for her performance on the uneven bar during the 1976 Olympics, where she won three gold medals, a silver, and a bronze. She returned to the 1980 Olympics, where she won two gold and two silver medals. She is a sportscast commentator for gymnastic events.

Bart Conner, an American gymnast who has won gold medals at every level of national and international competition, including the Olympics. He is a sportscast commentator for gymnastic events.

Nicole Rich, Rebecca's teammate and biggest rival, who always finishes first and tries very hard to be Rebecca's friend.

Kristy Cordice, Rebecca's bubbly, excitable teammate, who wants very much to win a medal.

Dylan Cordice, Kristy's eleven-year-old brother, who is T. J.'s best friend.

Coach Pruitt, the chief coach of the girls' gymnastic team.

Tess, a wise, supervising angel, who always says exactly what she thinks. She is sent by God to help Rebecca's mother restore balance to the Browner family. This time, she appears as a TV producer.

Monica, a loving, compassionate angel, whose special gift is truth. She is sent by God to help Rebecca remember what her father taught her about competing and what her Heavenly Father said about real love. This time, she appears as an assistant to the coach.

Andrew, an angel with a very special job. He is sent by God to watch over T. J. This time, he appears as the manager of the skate park.

Introduction

Monica frowned thoughtfully at the gymnastics bars. This was going to be a difficult assignment.

"Don't worry, Angel Girl," Tess chuckled. "You'll know what to do when the time comes. It's all a matter of balance . . . a very delicate balance."

Monica smiled back at her wise supervisor. "What puzzles me is why they do it, Tess. Spinning and jumping and flipping. And trying to be better at it than anyone else."

"That's not really what it's about, baby," said Tess. "Real champions aren't trying to beat someone *else*. They're just trying to be the best *they* can be. But sometimes people forget that."

"So that's why we were sent? To help them remember?" asked Monica.

Tess grew very serious. "Oh, our job is a lot bigger than that. But we'll have plenty of help. Andrew's here, too."

Introduction

"Andrew, the Angel of Death? Oh Tess, does that mean . . . ?"

Tess smiled serenely. "We don't know, baby. It's all in God's hands."

Chapter One

Arrivals and Rivals

Rebecca unpacked her special treasures and tried to make the small motel room feel like home. She held back a yawn. They'd driven all night to be here, and she was tired. But she wouldn't let it show. Winners don't get tired! They don't have time. Speaking of time. . . .

"Practice starts at noon, Mom. I've got to be right on time or Nicole's going to be there first and hog the bars like she always does!"

As Rebecca's mother, Sandra Browner, checked her watch, there was a knock at the door. It was Rebecca's teammates Nicole and Kristy. And they were bursting with news.

"Guess what?" asked a breathless Kristy, who got excited about everything, "Shelly Kramer's out!"

"What?" cried Rebecca, not sure if she was concerned or thrilled.

"She was doing back flips on the bars—" Kristy began.

"Without a spotter," added Nicole.

"And she fell and tore a tendon!" finished Kristy in a rush.

"Oh, that's too bad," said Mrs. Browner.

"I know," Kristy agreed, looking just a little guilty. Then she grinned at Rebecca, "Last time she beat you out of second place. Now it looks like you'll get second. And I'll have a shot at third!"

"But Nicole's still in first place," said Rebecca, frowning at the talented gymnast who made everything look so easy.

Nicole didn't notice. "Poor Shelly," she said. "What a tough break, missing the biggest meet of the year."

Just then Kristy's brother dashed into the room. "Really, Dylan!" said Kristy, trading "big sister" looks with Rebecca. "Don't you ever knock?"

"Oh, sorry," said Dylan, who wasn't really sorry at all. "Hi, Mrs. Browner. Where's T. J.?"

Dylan was eleven and just as noisy and pesky as Rebecca's little brother. *Which is probably why,* she thought, *he and T. J. are such good buddies!*

"Hey, Dylan," said T. J., banging the bathroom door into the wall. "What's happening?"

Dylan couldn't wait to tell him. "There's a skate park here. Nicole's mom is taking all the Nobodies. Wanna go?"

"I wish you kids wouldn't call each other Nobodies," said Rebecca and T. J.'s mom.

"Why not?" flashed Rebecca. "That's what they are."

"Dad didn't think so," said T. J., pretending her words didn't hurt at all.

"Subject closed," said their mom firmly. "You can go, T. J. Just be back by six so we can all have dinner together."

As the door slammed behind the boys, Rebecca looked at Kristy. And Kristy looked at Rebecca. Then they both began to grin and scream: "She tore a tendon!"

Nicole shook her head. "I don't believe you two!"

Practice started off with a surprise that afternoon. Coach Pruitt had a new assistant. "This is Monica. She's here to help us get ready for nationals. Her job is to make sure we have good, safe workouts. We don't want any more accidents like Shelly Kramer's!"

The slender young woman with the dancing eyes smiled at the girls, and they smiled back. All except Rebecca, who was already thinking about her first routine.

"We've got a lot to do in the next two days," Coach went on. "Push yourselves, but not too far. Practice, but not too hard. And be sure to ask for help if you need it. Remember, if anyone else gets hurt, I might have to get into leotards myself. And that won't be a pretty sight!"

As the giggling girls ran off to practice, Coach Pruitt turned to Monica. "Three of our girls are really feeling the pressure this week. Kristy Cordice came really close to third in the last meet. She could make a dangerous mistake, just because she's so darn excited."

He looked over at Nicole, who had just landed a perfect vault. "Nicole Rich has worked long and hard to stay on top. She could lose ground if she relaxes too much."

Then he glanced at Rebecca. A worried frown crossed his face. "But the one we need to keep an eye on is Rebecca Browner. That girl never lets up!"

"Is it true she's never fallen?" asked Monica.

Coach Pruitt nodded. "Never in competition."

Monica looked thoughtful. "That's a tough record to live up to."

"She wants to win, even if it kills her," he said. "And if she's not careful, it might."

Just then the noisy room grew very quiet. Every eye flew to the door as a television crew walked in. Leading the way was Tess—who liked nothing better than being in charge.

Leave it to Tess . . . , thought Monica with a grin, *she's always right in the thick of things!*

But it wasn't Tess who the dazzled, young gymnasts were staring at. She was just a television producer. But with her—ah, with her—were Nadia Comaneci and Bart Conner! The two Olympic champions were here as sportscast commentators reporting on the meet! Everyone in the gym knew about them. Even

Rebecca forgot about practicing as she watched her two heroes.

Nadia Comaneci, originally from Romania, was not only the first gymnast to receive a perfect score during an Olympic event, but she also won three gold medals, a silver, and a bronze in 1976. In the next Olympics, she won two gold medals and two silver medals. Bart Conner is the only American gymnast to win gold medals at every level of national or international competition.

And to top it all off, the two had married. *How romantic,* thought Rebecca. But when they walked over to Nicole, Rebecca shrugged and turned away.

Monica could see how much Rebecca wished she were the one getting all the attention. "They'll be covering the finals all week," she said cheerfully. "I'm sure they'll want to talk to all the girls."

Rebecca chalked her hands for a long time before she answered. "My mom says they only want to talk to winners." Then she tossed her head like it didn't matter at all and swung up onto the bars.

Chapter Two

Nobodies from Nowhere

As T. J. and Dylan laced on their Rollerblades, they looked around the busy skate park. "Awesome!" they agreed. They could barely wait to try out every bend, bank, pipe, and loop. It looked fast, noisy, and more than a little risky. Everything T. J. liked best!

They didn't mind a bit being the youngest kids there. They just ignored the teasing and waited for their turn.

"Show 'em your stuff, T. J.," said Dylan as his buddy stepped onto the track. T. J. intended to do just that.

"Hey, midget, where's your helmet?" called a big teenager.

"Don't need a helmet," said T. J., pushing off down the steep slope.

"Yes, you do," laughed the bigger boy, as he tossed his helmet right in front of T. J.'s speeding skates. There was no way to miss it, and T. J. didn't. His feet flew up in the air. He bounced off the wall and came down with a thump . . . all of which the older boys thought was very funny.

"Hey, what's the problem?" asked Andrew, in a deep voice, as he stepped onto the track.

"This 'little boy' fell down," said the teenager, as if he had no idea how it happened. Andrew gave him a long look. Then he reached down and helped T. J. to his feet.

"I'm okay," said T. J., pulling away.

"You the new man around here?" challenged the older boy. Then he took a really good look at Andrew and changed his mind.

"Yes, I am," said Andrew. "And if I see you putting somebody in danger again, you're out of here." Then he turned to T. J. "Come with me."

Much as he wanted to, T. J. didn't argue. He and Dylan just followed Andrew to the desk. But when Andrew opened a drawer and pulled out a first aid kit, T. J. spoke up. "I don't need anything. I'm gonna be fine."

"Yes, you are," agreed Andrew, "because we're going to make sure that elbow doesn't get infected, and because you're going to wear safety gear from now on. Helmet, knee pads, and elbow pads; or you don't skate here."

T. J. scowled. *Who'd have thought such a cool-looking guy would be such a stick-in-the-mud!*

"Darn," said Andrew, standing up, "no tape. Hang on a second, guys. I'll be right back." And he walked into a back room. While they waited, T. J. glanced into the open desk drawer and saw a cashbox! Almost without thinking, he reached inside and took a twenty-dollar bill.

Dylan couldn't believe his eyes. "What are you doing?" he whispered.

Before T. J. could answer, Andrew was back.

"You guys aren't from around here, are you?" he said, working on T. J.'s elbow.

"We're Nobodies from Nowhere," said T. J.

"Actually, we're from everywhere," Dylan explained. "Our sisters are gymnasts. We travel around with them."

"Yeah," put in T. J., "whether we like it or not."

Andrew smiled at Dylan. "Sounds like you enjoy it a little more than he does."

T. J. didn't have time for this. "Let's get outta here," he said to Dylan. And he was on his way out the door, followed by a worried Dylan. Andrew watched the boys leave, then opened the cashbox. He looked inside and knowingly shook his head.

Over in the practice gym, Monica was shaking her head, too. She'd tried all afternoon to make friends with Rebecca, but she knew her help wasn't welcome. The stubborn young girl had made that very clear as they worked on the same move over and over.

Monica handed Rebecca a towel and a bottle of water. "How about a break?"

Rebecca shook her head impatiently. "I didn't land exactly right. I want to do it again."

"Rebecca, you landed perfectly," said Monica. "The only thing missing was a smile."

"This is just practice, Monica. Smiles are for competition." Rebecca took the water and walked away.

Oh, Rebecca, thought Monica sadly, *where's your joy in what you can do?*

On the other side of town, T. J. and Dylan were climbing out of a taxi. "That'll be eight dollars," said the driver. T. J. handed him the stolen twenty-dollar bill.

So this is why he took the money, thought Dylan. *But why here? It's just an empty old house.* Even the "For Sale" sign in the ragged little yard looked tired to Dylan, but he followed T. J. up the front walk. "I still don't know why we're here." T. J. didn't answer. He just walked slowly around the house, looking through windows into empty rooms. "There's nobody here, T. J.!"

But T. J. didn't answer. He just kept going, until he came to the garage. Then he stopped, stood very still, and stared at the door.

What's the big deal? thought Dylan. *It's just an old garage door.*

But that's not what T. J. saw. He was remembering another time—a better time. It

15

was like he was there again. He had been only seven then. He'd really messed up his bike—and himself—but his dad could fix anything!

"It's okay, T. J.," his father, Peter Browner, had said. "As soon as we straighten this wheel, it'll be good as new."

"I don't want to get back on it," T. J. had said in a small voice. He had been scared he'd fall again.

Then his dad had knelt down and put his arm around him. "You can't give up every time you have an accident. If you fall, you get right back up and do it again." Then he had hugged T. J. "Don't worry. I'll always be there for you, pal. Promise."

T. J. started to smile. Then—suddenly—his thoughts were back to the present again, and his dad *wasn't* there for him. His dad *hadn't* kept his promise. He had died . . . *Dad died!*

All at once T. J. was furious—at everything and everybody. He felt like he was going to explode! He didn't know what to do. Then he saw a big rock in the flower bed. Without thinking, he picked it up and threw it as hard as he could—right through the front window!

"What are you doing, T. J.?!" yelped Dylan. "You can't throw rocks at houses!"

"You can if it's *your* house. You can do whatever you want!" yelled T. J. With tears rolling down his face, T. J. turned and ran down the street.

A very stunned Dylan followed him. He'd never seen T. J. cry before!

Neither boy noticed Andrew, who had been standing right there in the driveway the whole time. But then, people only see Andrew when God wants them to see him.

Chapter Three

Calling All Sponsors

Sandra Browner tugged on the phone cord, trying to make it reach into the motel bathroom. It was still early, and she didn't want to wake Rebecca and T. J. More importantly, she didn't want Rebecca to hear that there was trouble.

She tried to speak quietly, but it wasn't easy. "Please don't drop Rebecca. Your sponsorship is what pays for her training. Without it, she'd have to quit."

She listened for a moment, then exploded. "Not good enough?"

Mrs. Browner realized she was shouting and quickly lowered her voice. "Rebecca works her heart out. She'll catch Nicole. You watch. They'll be putting gold around her neck at the next Olympics."

Then she took a big breath and tried again. "Can we at least keep your company name on her outfits until we find another sponsor?" She looked over at her sleeping children. "So we don't look like losers . . . with no backing."

But Rebecca wasn't asleep. She'd heard every word. And as she lay there, eyes shut tight, a single tear crept out and ran down her cheek.

Rebecca couldn't seem to keep her mind on practice that day. Her eyes kept going to the pay phone in the corner. She watched as her mother made call after call.

Monica asked what was wrong. But Rebecca didn't want to talk about anything but work. "I have to practice. I have to get this right!"

T. J. waited impatiently while his mother finished another call. "Yes, I understand," she said. "You're only interested in one girl. Yes . . . Nicole *is* very talented."

As Mrs. Browner hung up with a sigh, T. J. grabbed his chance.

"Mom . . . ?"

"Not now, T. J.," said Mrs. Browner, looking through her address book. "Can't you see I'm busy?"

"I just want to go skating. Come watch me, Mom. You never do anything with me anymore."

"Oh, honey," said Mrs. Browner, "I can't. You go ahead. Just be back in an hour."

"Two hours," T. J. bargained.

"One," said Mrs. Browner. "No negotiation."

"Right," grumbled T. J., walking away, "we save *that* for Rebecca's sponsors."

T. J. was still mad when he got to the skate park. But he cheered up when he saw how quiet things were. He'd get plenty of time on the track today! First, though, there was something he had to do.

He waited for his chance. Finally, Andrew went into the back room. T. J. ran over and dropped a crumpled five-dollar bill on the counter near the cashbox. There, that was done. He turned around—and was face to face with Andrew! T. J.'s mouth dropped open.

"Taxi fares really add up, don't they?" said Andrew.

"How did you . . . ?" began an amazed T. J.

"Putting a rock through that window wasn't very cool," Andrew continued. "But I do understand how angry you are about your dad. Sometimes, even good memories can hurt."

T. J.'s eyes got very big. How could Andrew *know* all that? "Who are you?"

"All you need to know is that I'm concerned about you, and I'm here to help." Then Andrew looked at T. J. very seriously. "And there is Someone Else who wants to help you, too."

"Yeah? Well, it's a little late for that now," said T. J., starting to walk away.

Andrew's voice stopped him in his tracks. "What are you going to do about this?" he asked, holding out the five-dollar bill. "You're fifteen dollars short."

T. J. tried the sheepish grin that usually worked with his mom. "You said you wanted to help. How about helping with this?"

"I intend to," said Andrew. Then he handed T. J. a broom.

"No skating 'til you work this off. It should take about four hours."

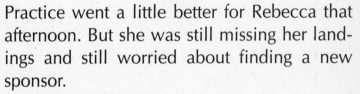

Practice went a little better for Rebecca that afternoon. But she was still missing her landings and still worried about finding a new sponsor.

Monica helped her up from the mat and looked across the gym at Rebecca's mom. "Your mother sure spends a lot of time on the phone."

"Maybe she wouldn't have to if I had a better dismount," said Rebecca.

"Do you really believe that?" asked Monica.

Rebecca shrugged her shoulders. Didn't Monica understand that sponsors only wanted the *best* girls?

"That's a lot of weight for a young girl to be carrying," said Monica, as if she had read her mind.

Rebecca looked at her with troubled eyes. Maybe Monica *could* help. Just then Nicole came into the gym—followed by three trainers and two photographers. *Great,* thought Rebecca, *the "Nicole Road Show" is back!*

Nicole called to Rebecca with a friendly smile, "Want to warm up with me?"

"I'm warm," snapped Rebecca, turning to the balance beam. She never noticed how hurt Nicole looked.

Monica couldn't help noticing that Rebecca was slipping farther away, and she wondered if Tess wouldn't have been a better angel for this job.

But Tess had her own job to do. "Need a quarter?" she asked, as Sandra Browner dug through her purse.

"Oh!" said a startled Mrs. Browner, "I didn't see you coming."

"That happens a lot," said Tess—with an angelic smile.

Then she got to work. "Tell me, Mrs. Browner, how does this sponsorship thing work? I thought amateur athletes couldn't accept money."

"Oh, they can't," said Mrs. Browner. "But companies can sponsor a girl's training. Then they get dibs on her when she turns pro. Sponsors make it possible for families like ours. Olympic gold is expensive."

"Sounds like you've got big plans for the future," said Tess.

"I've got it all worked out," said Mrs. Browner confidently.

"Tomorrow, maybe," agreed Tess as she handed her a quarter, "but what about today?"

Chapter
Four

Missing in Action

Mrs. Browner couldn't stop thinking about Tess's question: *What about today?* She was doing her best for her family! Wasn't she? Then she shrugged her shoulders. She couldn't worry about this now. She had to go round up T. J.,who was late again.

"T. J.," she called sharply, as she walked into the skate park. "I told you one hour. Why are you still here?" Then Mrs. Browner noticed what he was doing. "And why are you sweeping the floor?"

Uh oh! thought T. J. Now he was in real trouble.

"He's paying back a debt," said Andrew.

T. J. knew he had to explain. "Mom, yesterday I . . ."

Andrew came to the rescue. "Yesterday he borrowed some money. I told him he could work it off."

Mrs. Browner was shocked. "Borrowed money? What did you need money for?" But she didn't wait for an answer. "Never mind. We'll discuss it later." She turned to Andrew. "How much does he owe you?"

"He's got it down to about ten dollars," Andrew answered. Mrs. Browner was very polite as she paid Andrew, but T. J. knew that look in her eyes. She was really mad! He kept very quiet—and thought very fast—all the way to the car.

Neither the quiet nor the thinking helped. By the time they reached the motel room, the battle was in full swing. "You borrowed the money for a movie? Give me a break, T. J.!"

T. J. was furious. "Why do you always think I'm lying?"

Mrs. Browner started to answer, then looked over at Rebecca. "Let's not have this argument right now."

"Why not?" snapped T. J. "Because it might upset Rebecca? Because this is *her* big week?" Then he looked his mother right in the eye. "Or because it's *your* big week?"

Sandra Browner felt like she'd been slapped. How could he say such a thing? But before she could answer him, the phone rang.

Even T. J. was shocked by what he'd said. He walked very slowly to the bed and sat down. Rebecca looked at her little brother—really looked at him—for a moment. Then she sat down beside him. "You didn't go to the movies, did you?" she asked quietly.

T. J. shook his head. "I went to the house. It's like Mom wants us to totally forget about Dad, but I want to remember." He looked at his sister hopefully. "Don't you?"

Rebecca's eyes filled with tears. Then she caught her breath and stood up very fast. "Not now. I have to focus." Without skipping a beat, she picked up her hand weights and started exercising.

"Rebecca, guess what!" called her mother. She sounded happier than she had in a long time. "Gibson Athletic Socks wants to talk about sponsoring you!" Mrs. Browner almost seemed to dance as she started for the door. "I'm meeting them in twenty minutes. They want to see you at two o'clock at the gym. Don't be late, sweetheart."

The small room was very quiet after their mom left. Then all at once, T. J. jumped up and grabbed his skates. "Where are you going?" asked Rebecca.

"What do you care?" said T. J. as he slammed out of the room.

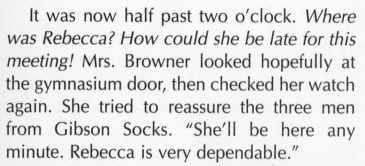

It was now half past two o'clock. *Where was Rebecca? How could she be late for this meeting!* Mrs. Browner looked hopefully at the gymnasium door, then checked her watch again. She tried to reassure the three men from Gibson Socks. "She'll be here any minute. Rebecca is very dependable."

But the three men were checking their watches, too, and they didn't look happy— especially Mr. McKenzie, who had the authority to approve or reject the sponsorship on the spot.

Mrs. Browner glanced at the door again. "Maybe she got the time wrong," she said nervously.

"That's too bad," said Mr. McKenzie. "I'm afraid we can't wait much longer. We have a three o'clock appointment . . . with Nicole Rich's parents."

"Oh," said Mrs. Browner. She knew what *that* meant, but she tried anyway. "Maybe tomorrow, then?"

Mr. McKenzie almost smiled. "Well, I suppose that depends on what happens with the Riches. It was nice meeting you."

"Oh . . . yes . . . thank you," said Mrs. Browner. She tried to hide her disappointment. She'd worked so hard for this opportunity! Now it was gone.

Where WAS Rebecca?!

Chapter Five

Perfect Memories

Rebecca meant to be at the gym on time. But had somehow, she'd felt drawn to the house that used to be home. She stood in the tall grass of the small yard. Remembering . . .

It seemed so long ago. She had been five and so determined to learn that handspring. She'd tried and tried. Then finally, she'd done one that was just a *little* wobbly. As she stood here now, her memory replayed her daddy's encouraging words. "Almost, honey . . . almost."

But Rebecca had never been satisfied with *almost.* "I want to do it perfectly!" she had told her dad.

Her father, Peter Browner, had smiled. "Nobody's perfect, baby."

But Rebecca knew that wasn't true. "Nadia Comaneci is perfect," she'd told him.

And that's when Daddy had gotten very serious. "Don't you worry about being any-body but *you!* That's who I love." Then he kissed her on the tip of her nose. "That's who

I'm always gonna love. Promise me you'll remember that, Becky."

"I promise, Daddy," she'd said, darting away to try another flip.

But had she remembered? Had she? Her eyes filled with tears. She brushed them away impatiently. What did it matter? That little girl was gone. And so was her daddy.

Suddenly Rebecca remembered something else. She looked at her watch. Oh, no! It was half past two o'clock! She turned and ran down the street.

By the time Rebecca rushed into the gym, practice was finished. The television crew was leaving, and almost everyone else was gone. Everyone except Monica and Rebecca's mother, who was on the telephone again.

When she saw her daughter, Mrs. Browner slammed down the phone.

"Rebecca, where have you been?"

Rebecca had never seen her mother so angry. "I . . . I went for a walk."

"A walk!" Mrs. Browner shouted. "You were supposed to be here!"

"I'm sorry, Mom."

Mrs. Browner's face was very red. "You're sorry! I had sponsors ready to hand you a contract. But you took a walk instead!"

Rebecca felt awful. "I'm . . . I'm sorry, Mom. Maybe you could call them or something—"

Mrs. Browner didn't even wait for her daughter to finish. "It's too late . . . too late." Her eyes filled with tears, and she grabbed her purse. "I'll see you at the motel. Right now I have to track down your brother."

Rebecca stood very still for a long time. She was sorry, and sad, and—for once—had no idea what to do next. Finally she just sat down.

"Are you okay?" asked Monica, coming over to sit beside her. Rebecca gave a nod.

"Actually," Monica went on in a soothing voice, "I think you should take *more* walks. Maybe with some friends like Kristy and Nicole. It would do you all good to get out in the fresh air."

Rebecca wasn't really listening. "I went home."

"Home?" repeated Monica.

Rebecca nodded again. "We used to live just a few miles from here, before my dad died. He had cancer."

Monica put a gentle hand on her shoulder. "I'm so sorry, Rebecca."

"Mom made us move out practically the next day. I mean . . . one day we were a family living in a house. Then all of a sudden we were like nomads living in motels." Rebecca had never talked about this before. But it felt okay to tell Monica.

"I kept telling myself we were just on a long trip to a meet. And when we got back home, Daddy would be waiting for us." Rebecca started to cry. "But he wasn't."

Monica held her closely as, one by one, the gym lights dimmed.

Then something wonderful happened—something Rebecca would never forget.

It had been a long day for Nadia Comaneci and Bart Conner. They'd interviewed excited, young gymnasts and taped background segments for the coming broadcast. Now they walked slowly toward the door. But as they crossed the practice area, they both stopped at the same time. They looked at each other, then at the empty gym—not noticing Rebecca and Monica in the corner—and smiled.

Bart made a sweeping bow to Nadia, then held out his hand. She laughed and answered with a deep curtsy. She spun around and—light as a feather—sprang up onto the balance beam. Bart waved and headed for the tumbling mats.

Rebecca held her breath and watched with glistening eyes as the two champions performed for no one but themselves—just for the joy of doing it! It was like a beautiful dance, she thought, to music only they could hear.

"Remember when all *you* thought about was the fun?" whispered Monica.

Rebecca never took her eyes from Nadia and Bart. "That was a long time ago."

"It's never too late to feel that way again," Monica promised.

Chapter
Six

T. J.'s Fast Track

As Nadia and Bart tumbled and leapt, T. J. was doing some "leaping" of his own. Fists clenched, eyes angry, he raced around the skate park course as fast as he could go. Shooting through pipes . . . skimming around curves . . . and doing flips off the top of every steep bank. But no matter how fast he went, he couldn't outrun his anger.

"T. J.!" yelled a scared Dylan, "where's your helmet?"

T. J. ignored him. He was tired of being a Nobody! Tired of feeling alone! Tired of missing his dad!

Andrew ran over. "T. J.! Come in right now!" But T. J. just skated faster. Too fast. At the top of the final loop, his skates shot right over the edge of the track. He tried to turn it into a flip, but it didn't work.

Time seemed to stop. T. J. hung upside down in the air for what felt like forever. Then he crashed to the concrete floor, head first.

Mrs. Browner arrived at the skate park, angry that T. J. was late *again*. What was wrong with her children! First Rebecca, now T. J. . . . always late! But where *was* T. J.? And what was everyone looking at over by the track?

Then she saw Dylan. "Where's T. J.?"

Dylan's voice shook. "I told him to put on his helmet, Mrs. Browner. But he wouldn't. . . ."

Sandra Browner looked at the silent crowd by the track. "Oh, no!" she gasped and ran toward the crowd. She pushed her way into the circle. There in Andrew's arms was T. J. covered in blood. Mrs. Browner was so stunned, she bearly heard the sound of the ambulance arriving to rush T. J. to the hospital.

Mrs. Browner sat by T. J.'s hospital bed, holding his hand. She'd forgotten how small her son was. His noisy energy had always filled any room he was in. Now he was so quiet. She touched his face gently. "Oh, T. J., please wake up. Come back to us, honey."

But T. J. didn't hear her. He was far away. And the doctors couldn't say when he'd wake up . . . or *if* he'd wake-up at all.

"Mrs. Browner, I'm so sorry." Andrew's voice was filled with regret. "I told T. J. to wear a helmet, but I should have watched him more closely. This is my fault."

"No, Andrew," she said sadly. "T. J. doesn't listen. He's been angry for a long time now." Her eyes filled with tears. "Ever since his dad died." Then she took a deep breath and sat up very straight. "It's kind of you to be here, but you really don't have to stay."

"Yes, I do," said Andrew in a very strange voice. "It's . . . part of my job."

Sandra Browner didn't understand what that really meant. She didn't know that Andrew was an angel—and that he had the special assignment of keeping a close eye on her son.

"It does help having you here," she said with a sigh.

"I've been so alone ever since my husband died." Her voice shook. "Oh, Andrew . . . first Peter and now T. J.!" Tears ran down her face.

"Mom?" said a scared voice from the doorway. "Mom? What happened to T. J.?" Rebecca walked in very slowly, staring at her little brother in the big bed.

"T. J. has a very serious head injury," said Andrew.

Rebecca looked at Andrew with frightened eyes. "Are you a doctor?"

Mrs. Browner put her arm around Rebecca. "No, honey, Andrew's a friend of T. J.'s." She hugged her daughter. "I'm so glad you're here." Mrs. Browner turned to Andrew. "Rebecca's the strong one in the family," she said with pride. "She never falls apart . . . she never falls at all."

Rebecca sat by T. J. all afternoon. She barely moved. She wasn't even sure she *could* move. It was like something very heavy was pushing down on her, squeezing all the breath out of her. But she couldn't give in to it! She didn't dare. She had to be strong.

Rebecca shook her head and stood up. "Mom, why don't you take a break? I'll stay with T. J."

Mrs. Browner tried to smile. "Thanks, honey. Maybe I'll take a little walk."

After her mother left, Rebecca pulled her chair closer to the bed. She had something very important to say to her brother. And all she could do was hope that—somewhere deep inside—he would hear her.

"T. J.," she said softly, "I went to the house. It looks so sad—like no one ever lived there." She took his hand. "But then I saw the garage door. Remember how Dad used to make those marks every time we grew? Remember what he always said?"

Then Rebecca leaned even closer to T. J. and used her best "big sister" voice. "Hey, buddy. I don't like that joke about 'Nobodies.' You're somebody to me. And, T. J., I promise I'll be a better sister from now on."

Chapter Seven

Leap of Faith

Mrs. Browner's walk took her all the way back to their old house, and it brought back memories for her, too.

She stood in the driveway, looking sadly at the ragged lawn, the peeling paint. Then she walked to the garage door and found the line of pencil marks. And, suddenly, she could see them all, just the way they used to be: Peter, laughing and teasing as he measured his growing family and added new marks. Rebecca in her leotard, a whole inch taller! And T. J. stretching up on tiptoe when he thought no one was looking.

But Peter never missed a thing his children did. "Don't try to be what you aren't, son," he'd said with a grin. "You're exactly as tall as you're supposed to be."

Mrs. Browner touched T. J.'s mark very softly and began to cry.

"Sandra Browner," a voice quietly said.

Mrs. Browner whirled around. Standing right beside her—in the space that was empty just a moment ago—was Tess! What was a television producer doing here?

Mrs. Browner quickly wiped away her tears. "I . . . I'm sorry. This isn't a good time for an interview."

Tess beamed at her. "Mrs. Browner, I have some really good news. I've found you a sponsor."

"You have?" Mrs. Browner was thrilled.

"That's right," said Tess. "God. And He wants to give you a little coaching. So He sent me. I'm an angel."

Sandra Browner stared at Tess and the soft, golden light that wrapped around her. This was crazy! But, somehow, she believed every word. Then, suddenly, she was angry. "I don't need an angel! My children do."

"They've got 'em," answered Tess. "And right now, so do you. We've got some serious talking to do," Tess added. And when Tess wanted to talk, people listened. She looked Sandra Browner straight in the eyes. "I want to talk about winning and the way you push your daughter. No matter how many gold medals Rebecca wins, it'll never make up for what you lost—who you lost."

Mrs. Browner began to cry. "I miss him so much."

Tess was sorry for Sandra Browner's pain, but there was more to this lesson. "Mrs. Browner, Peter left you a home to live in and a family to love." She glanced at the house. "But you ran away. And you've used Rebecca's career as an excuse—an excuse to keep from facing the truth."

Then her voice grew very gentle. "Your husband is gone, but that doesn't mean that this house is empty. Or that you won't see him again."

Mrs. Browner raised tear-filled eyes. "I keep looking for the faith in God to believe that."

"God says if you have faith as small as a mustard seed . . . nothing will be impossible for you,"[1] said Tess. "So, don't *look*, baby. Leap!" Tess's smile was warm enough to melt the coldest heart. "It's like those flying leaps Rebecca takes from one bar to another.

There's a second there when you're not hanging on to anything . . . and it's very scary. But that's when God will hold you up. Remember, He is with you."[2]

Then the light around Tess grew even brighter. "He'll hold you up right now. Now. This shining moment between past and future—that's what *now* is, baby. That's where you are. And that's where you've got to start living—for yourself and your children."

Mrs. Browner closed her eyes for a moment. Could it really *be* that simple? She took a shaky breath and looked up. But suddenly she was alone. Tess was gone—just like that—but she didn't feel alone anymore.

When Sandra Browner returned to her son's hospital room, Rebecca could hardly believe it was her mother. Her mom's eyes were shining, and she looked so . . . so different. The tired worried look was gone. "Mom? Are you okay?"

"Oh yes, sweetheart, I'm very okay." Mrs. Browner took her daughter's hands in hers. "But I'm afraid I'll have to disappoint you. You know I never miss any of your competitions. But tomorrow I can't be there. I have to stay with T. J."

"I know, Mom. And I promise I'll do my best. I'll win . . ." Rebecca looked over at the bed, "for T. J."

But Mrs. Browner shook her head. "No, honey, don't do it for T. J. And don't do it for me." Then she squeezed Rebecca's hands very tight. "Rebecca, don't do it at all unless it's what you want. I mean it, baby. I want what's best for you. For you, Rebecca."

What she wanted? Rebecca just stared at her mother. She had never been so confused. What did she want? No one had asked Rebecca that question in a long time. Including Rebecca herself.

Chapter Eight

The Competition

Every seat in the huge arena was filled. And the audience buzzed with excitement as the young gymnasts warmed up. Nationals were about to start!

Tess gave the signal to the TV crew, and the cameras came on. "Today's top story has to be Rebecca Browner," Bart Conner said gravely. "Her brother is in a coma in a local hospital. And no one knows how this will affect her performance."

Nadia nodded. "That little girl's got a lot on her shoulders today, Bart."

Rebecca didn't know people were hearing her name all over America. And she didn't care. She had just one thing on her mind—winning.

Rebecca jumped as a small hand touched her shoulder. "How's T. J. doing?" asked Nicole with concern.

"Is he gonna be okay?" asked a worried Kristy.

Rebecca shrugged. "It's my problem. Don't worry about it."

Nicole usually ignored Rebecca's rudeness. But this made her mad! "We care, okay. So it is our problem."

Rebecca's chin went up. "Yeah, well I don't want to take your mind off the meet."

Kristy had had enough, too. "Chill, Rebecca. She's only trying to help."

"I don't need anyone's help," said Rebecca coldly.

Nicole tried again. "Look, I know you're mad about the Gibson Socks thing . . ."

Kristy nudged Nicole and said, ". . . and the fact that *you're* ranked first."

"That's right," said Nicole, who never— ever—bragged. "And I wouldn't be, if it weren't for hard work, my family, and . . ." she looked Rebecca right in the eye, "*friends!*"

Coach Pruitt stepped in to make peace. "Okay ladies, we're all a little tense. And we're all worried about T. J. So let's do something that *can* help. Let's say a prayer for him."

He looked around at the bowed heads. They were good kids, and he was proud of every one of them. But they still had things to learn. "God, help us to never forget our families and to take good care of them. Because when the glitz and applause are over, they're all we have left," he prayed softly.

Then Coach Pruitt clapped his hands and gave his team a big smile. "Okay! Now let's get out there and show our stuff!"

Rebecca stood with her team while the "Star Spangled Banner" played, but she felt all alone. It was like she was inside a very thin bubble made of ice. No one could get inside with her, but that was the way she wanted it. Wasn't it? If you let people get close, sooner or later they'd go away. Like Daddy . . . and maybe T. J.

But she couldn't think about that now. She couldn't! So Rebecca quit thinking and just let her body take over and do what she'd practiced so hard to do. And she was good. Very, very good. But so were her rivals—especially Kristy and Nicole.

The Competition

Kristy had nailed all her landings on the vault and had a real shot at second place. And Nicole's skill and grace brought the crowd to its feet as she finished each routine. Nicole was very close to taking first place again. But there was still room for Rebecca to win!

"It's all coming down to the wire," Nadia told the TV audience. "There's just one event left. And the overall scores are so close it's hard to say who will win."

Bart nodded. "The difference is going to be who stays on the balance beam and who sticks their landings."

Tess leaned close to the microphone and whispered something. Nadia touched her earphones, listened for a moment, then smiled as she repeated Tess's words. "Just like life, Bart: Keep your balance and land on your feet."

Chapter Nine

Moment of Truth

A hush fell over the arena as Rebecca walked to the balance beam. She was the last to compete, and her performance would decide the championship.

Rebecca knew it, too, and suddenly, that icy little bubble broke. Everything came rushing in. Daddy . . . T. J. . . . all the hard work.

Her hands started to shake, and she couldn't seem to breathe.

Monica walked over and put a hand on her shoulder. "Rebecca?"

But Rebecca didn't hear her. She stared at the narrow strip of wood. It was like a bridge. And at the other end was everything she wanted. She shook off Monica's hand and took a deep breath. She could do this. She *would* do this!

Rebecca put her hands on the beam—*don't fall. Don't fall.* She sprang into a forward roll and stood up. She arched her back, pointed an elegant toe, and began her routine.

It was a little wobbly at first. But with each spin, somersault, and leap, Rebecca's moves grew stronger, surer. And she was dancing—flying!—as she soared into the back flip that was T. J.'s favorite. *T. J.! Oh, T. J.!*

It all came apart then. And Rebecca—the girl who *never* fell—was falling. She seemed to fall forever, and when she hit the mat at last, she was all by herself. Just Rebecca, lying in a pool of brilliant light in a dark, empty place. She could no longer see or hear the crowd.

Then, there on the balance beam—looking perfectly at peace—stood Monica. But *this* Monica didn't look at all like a coach's assistant. Her long, shimmery dress might have been spun from moonbeams. And she . . . she . . . seemed to glow!

"What's happening?" asked a shocked Rebecca. "I can't believe it. I don't fall. I don't."

"Well you did, Rebecca. You slipped and you fell," came Monica's voice. "Now stand up."

Rebecca sighed. "It's too late. I've lost."

Monica shook her head. "It's not the winning or the losing, Rebecca,"—and her words seemed to sing—"it's the getting up that counts." Then she smiled and raised one eyebrow. "Isn't that what your father always said?"

"How did you know that?" None of this made any sense to Rebecca, but the familiar words were comforting.

"God knows, and He told me," answered Monica, drifting down to kneel beside her.

"I'm an angel, Rebecca," she said. "God sent me to be here with you when you fell."[3]

Rebecca was starting to get very scared. "Why would an angel come when I fall?"

Monica smiled at her. "Can you think of a better time for an angel to show up?" Her eyes sparkled. "People tend to see things differently when they need help."

Maybe Monica *was* an angel. And if she was . . . "What's going to happen to T. J.?" Rebecca asked anxiously. "Will he be all right?"

"I don't know if he will live," said Monica gently, "but I do know he will be all right. Everyone in this world has to get up and go on every day without knowing what's going to happen. People can never be sure how long they'll have those they love."

Then Monica looked at Rebecca very intently. This was important. "But one thing is certain, Rebecca. No one is ever alone, because God is *always* there. T. J.'s not alone. And you won't be alone on that beam."

The beam . . . the competition! Rebecca looked around. "Where is everybody?"

"They're here," said Monica calmly, "waiting for you to get up. Even your rivals want you to get up. Because they're your friends, too. And you've got all the time in the world to decide whether or not you will."

Then Monica smiled at the bewildered girl. "Personally, I think you should get up. God thinks you should. And your father would think so, too. But it's your choice."

This was all too much for Rebecca. "My father?"

Monica nodded. "Peter is very proud of you."

Rebecca shook her head, holding back her tears. "He's dead."

"He's in the presence of God, Rebecca. And you are, too." Monica's voice was like music. "And there is something you need to hear in this special moment that God has created for you. God loves you, little one. And He gave you a good and kind father, not for a long time, but for enough time."

Monica reached out and lifted Rebecca's chin, looking deep into her eyes. "Time enough," she repeated, "to teach you and your brother the lessons you need . . . not to win, but to grow. Peter taught you always to do your best . . . to live and play and love with all your heart and soul."

Rebecca's tears overflowed. "But I didn't," she sobbed. "When it mattered most, I didn't!"

And as Monica held her in her loving arms, Rebecca poured out all the hurt. "When Daddy was dying, I was afraid. And the sicker he got, the more scared I got. And the harder it was, the more I stayed away and practiced instead. I just kept putting off going to see him . . . until . . . it was too late."

Rebecca cried like her heart would break. "I never said good-bye to Daddy, Monica. I never said good-bye."

Monica held her very tight for a moment. Then opened her arms and stood up. "Rebecca, you don't have to say good-bye!" She smiled warmly at the astonished girl. "What if you just say 'til we meet again? What if you choose to stand up and show everyone what your father taught you? That's the best farewell you could ever give him."

Rebecca sat very still in the light. Then she lifted her head, slowly wiped the tears from her face, and stood up.

Suddenly, time moved again. Rebecca was back in the crowded arena. And everyone was clapping. For her! *Just for standing up?* she thought. *Well, I can do a lot better than that!*

Rebecca walked proudly to the beam to finish what she'd started. She'd lost her chance to win, but that didn't matter. suddenly this was about something a lot more important than winning.

Rebecca had never felt so light and free. Every move flowed into the next with grace and ease . . . and joy. Then when she spun through her flying dismount—landing with perfect balance, the crowd jumped to its feet!

But Rebecca didn't even notice the standing ovation. Her eyes were lifted to heaven. She smiled as she raised a slender arm and waved good-bye.

Then, slicing through the storm of applause, came a joyful "Whoop" from Tess—who could always be heard when she wanted to be. "T. J. just woke up!" she sang out.

Rebecca flashed a brilliant smile at Monica. "And so did I," she said.

Her teammates ran up and surrounded her, and she didn't mind the hugs at all!

"Unbelievable," said a bouncing Kristy.

"That was awesome!" Nicole beamed at her.

Rebecca looked at Nicole in surprise. "I could beat you next time, you know. And you're still happy for me?"

"Of course," said Nicole. Then added, with a teasing smile, "Some of my best friends are champions."

Rebecca's answering smile was bright enough to light up the room. She threw her arms around Nicole and Kristy. "My best friends are, too."

Chapter Ten

The Road Home

Mrs. Browner carefully made a mark on the garage door. "Stand up straight, Rebecca. We're going to be keeping track of this for a long time." Sandra Browner and her daughter smiled as they watched T. J. pull the "For Sale" sign from the yard.

Then, arms around each other, the Browner family walked into the little house. They'd come home to stay!

Across town in the silent gym, three angels were about to go home, too. But first . . .

Tess winked at Andrew. "Okay, Miss Wings," she said to Monica, pointing to the parallel bars. "Let's see what you've learned."

"The first thing I learned," said Monica, digging both hands into a big bowl of talc, "is always chalk . . . up!" And she swept a handful of talc into the air!

Monica laughed and put her arms around them both. Together they watched as the cloud of chalk dust swirled and danced in the still air. Spiraling up . . . and up. Higher . . . and higher. Until—with a sweep of shining wings—a snow white dove soared toward heaven.

Endnotes

1. Matthew 17:20.
2. Isaiah 41:10.
3. Psalm 37:24.

Join Tess, Monica, and Andrew in another
Touched By An Angel **book.**

Have You Seen Me
(an excerpt)

Sarah tossed and turned. It was very late, but she couldn't get to sleep. Even thinking about that new mystery by her favorite writer didn't help. And Sarah loved figuring out the answer before the end of the book! But she couldn't be bothered with a made-up story tonight. She had a mystery of her own to solve . . . right here at home.

She threw back the covers, picked up her big flashlight, and crept down to the kitchen. Opening the refrigerator, she stood staring at the milk carton photo that looked so much— so very much—like her brother, Noah. But that couldn't be! Could it?